"A beautifully illustrated tale of how children may experience a stormy divorce. *The Storm* o
guidance about learning to manage the difficult feelings within the ensuing turmoil."

Hephzibah Kaplan, Art Therapist, Director of

"*The Storm* is a powerful story about parental separation, and could be used with both children and parents together, to help parents understand the impact of the conflict in their relationships on their children, allowing for open conversations. *The Storm* could encourage sharing of worries and fears and give children a sense of safety in talking about their experiences with professionals who are supporting children through a scary and uncertain period in their lives."

Sarah-Jane Farr, Family Support Keyworker, Early Help WSCC

"A beautifully written and illustrated book that can help young children explore and acknowledge difficult emotions such as guilt, sadness and anger that may be experienced through parental separation. It helps dispel the myth that children are to blame whilst reassuring children that they are still loved by each parent even though their parents no longer love each other."

Janey Treharne, Jigsaw, South East

"The power of these stories lies in their deeper natural and archetypal metaphor, something like the deeper Mother Earth continuity below any surface. Before even reading any of these *Therapeutic Fairy Tales*, you feel their tenderness through the stunningly beautiful illustrations."

Molly Wolfe, Art Psychotherapist, Sandplay Specialist

The Storm

This beautifully illustrated and sensitive storybook is designed to be used therapeutically by professionals and caregivers supporting children whose parents are going through a separation. With engaging and colourful illustrations that can be used to prompt conversation, it tells the story of a Brother and Sister who are helped to come to terms with the new, changing shape of their family.

This book is also available to buy as part of the *Therapeutic Fairy Tales* set. *Therapeutic Fairy Tales* is a series of short modern tales dedicated to exploring challenging situations that might be faced by children. Each short story is designed to be used by professionals and parents as they use stories therapeutically to support children's mental and emotional health.

Other books in the series include:

- *Storybook Manual: Introduction To Working With Storybooks Therapeutically And Creatively*
- *The Night Crossing: A Lullaby For Children On Life's Last Journey*
- *The Island: For Children With A Parent Living With Depression*

Designed to be used with children aged 6 and above, each story has an accompanying online resource, offering therapeutic prompts and creative exercises to support the practitioner. These resources can also be adapted for wider use with siblings and other family members.

The Storm – part of the *Therapeutic Fairy Tales* series – is born out of a creative collaboration between Pia Jones and Sarah Pimenta.

Pia Jones is an author, workshop facilitator and UKCP integrative arts psychotherapist, who trained at The Institute for Arts in Therapy & Education. Pia has worked with children and adults in a variety of school, health and community settings. Core to her practice is using arts and story as support during times of loss, transition and change, giving a TEDx talk on the subject. She was Story Director on artgym's award-winning film documentary, 'The Moving Theatre,' where puppetry brought to life real stories of people's migrations. Pia also designed the 'Sometimes I Feel' story cards, a Speechmark therapeutic resource to support children with their feelings. You can view her work at www.silverowlartstherapy.com

Sarah Pimenta is an experienced artist, workshop facilitator and lecturer in creativity. Her specialist art form is print-making, and her creative practice has brought texture, colour and emotion into a variety of environments, both in the UK and abroad. Sarah has over 20 years' experience of designing and delivering creative, high-quality art workshops in over 250 schools, diverse communities and public venues, including the British Library, V&A, NESTA, Oval House and many charities. Her work is often described as art with therapeutic intent, and she is skilled in working with adults and children who have access issues and complex needs. Sarah is known as Social Fabric, www.social-fabric.co.uk

Both Pia and Sarah hope these *Therapeutic Fairy Tales* open up conversations that enable children and families' own stories and feelings to be seen and heard.

Therapeutic Fairy Tales

Pia Jones and Sarah Pimenta

978-0-367-25108-6

This unique therapeutic book series includes a range of beautifully illustrated and sensitively written fairy tales to support children who are experiencing trauma, distress and challenging experiences, as well as a manual designed to support the therapeutic use of story.

Titles in the series include:

Storybook Manual: An Introduction To Working With Storybooks Therapeutically And Creatively
978-0-367-49117-8

The Night Crossing: A Lullaby For Children On Life's Last Journey
978-0-367-49120-8

The Island: For Children With A Parent Living With Depression
978-0-367-49198-7

The Storm: For Children Growing Through Parents' Separation
978-0-367-49196-3

The Storm

For Children Growing Through Parents' Separation

Pia Jones and Sarah Pimenta

Routledge
Taylor & Francis Group

LONDON AND NEW YORK

First published 2021
by Routledge
2 Park Square, Milton Park, Abingdon, Oxon OX14 4RN

and by Routledge
52 Vanderbilt Avenue, New York, NY 10017

Routledge is an imprint of the Taylor & Francis Group, an informa business

British Library Cataloguing-in-Publication Data
A catalogue record for this book is available from the British Library

Library of Congress Cataloging-in-Publication Data
Names: Jones, Pia, author. | Pimenta, Sarah, illustrator.
Title: The storm : for children growing through parents' separation / Pia Jones and Sarah Pimenta.
Description: New York, NY : Routledge, 2020. | Series: Therapeutic fairy tales | Summary: When their house splits in two with one parent on either side, Brother and Sister fall into the crack between them but are helped by a firebird to come to terms with the new situation. Includes a note on how to use the book as a therapeutic resource.
Identifiers: LCCN 2020002065 (print) | LCCN 2020002066 (ebook) | ISBN 9780367491949 (hardback) | ISBN 9780367491963 (paperback) | ISBN 9781003044987 (ebook)
Subjects: CYAC: Family problems--Fiction.
Classification: LCC PZ7.1.J726 Sto 2020 (print) | LCC PZ7.1.J726 (ebook) | DDC [E]--dc23
LC record available at https://lccn.loc.gov/2020002065
LC ebook record available at https://lccn.loc.gov/2020002066

ISBN: 978-0-367-49196-3 (pbk)
ISBN: 978-1-003-04498-7 (ebk)

Typeset in Calibri and Antitled
by Servis Filmsetting, Stockport, Cheshire

Visit the eResources: www.routledge.com/9780367491963

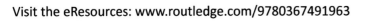

Acknowledgements

A special thank you to Stuart Lynch for all the time and creative support he generously gave to *The Storm*. Thanks to Hephzibah Kaplan for her enriching input and ideas.

Thanks to Speechmark for looking after our fairy tales so well and turning them into such beautiful books. A special mention also to our editor, Katrina Hulme-Cross, for her calm, steady guidance, and enthusiastic support for these stories. And to Leah Burton, Cathy Henderson and Alison Jones for taking our books into production with such care and attention.

Thanks to all the other people who have supported us along the journey: Alastair Bailey, Tamsin Cooke, Katrina Hillkirk, Molly Wolfe, Fiamma Ceccomori-Jones, Sarah Farr, Jacob Pimenta-Richardson, Daniele Ceccomori, Antonella Mancini and Alex Poole.

A word of caution

Before starting *The Storm*, please take a moment to read below

The Storm has been especially written for children with parents going through separation and divorce. The storybook is designed to serve as a therapeutic resource to support children with their personal, emotional journeys, to generate discussion and reflection alongside an adult reader.

Given the sensitive subject matter, it is essential the story is read in the right setting, with respect and due care for the child's well-being, leaving plenty of time for reactions, feelings and thoughts. This is not a story that can be rushed.

For the adult reader, professional or non-professional, it is advisable to read this story first alone, to ensure you have time to process your emotions in order to prepare for therapeutic work with your child reader.

For extra resources on how to work with this story, and examples of creative exercises, please go to the online resources: www.routledge.com/9780367491963. For ideas on how to work with story and image in general, please refer to our *Storybook Manual: An Introduction To Working With Storybooks Therapeutically And Creatively*: www.routledge.com/9780367491178.

Once upon a time there lived a family in a twisty old treehouse, a Brother and Sister with their parents.

Every day after school, the children would rush home to play, climb and make dens in the tallest branches. Their parents were just as busy, working hard to build a family life.

But the air crackled with stresses, old and new. Sometimes the children heard their parents stop and sharpen their voices.

"You never ... why don't you ... you're always ... how could you," rustled through the branches before being blown away.

With a quick frown, the Sister and Brother tried to carry on. With games to invent, life to live, they could almost ignore the storm-cloud growing, the leaves whispering. Still the cloud grew bigger, whipping up their parents' hurts and voices, stirring them round, turning them louder.

It was only when Mum and Dad began to throw words like rocks or withdrew them altogether, the children knew it – their parents' languages were no longer the same.

"What's going on?" whispered the Sister to her Brother. "Mum and Dad fight more than us."

"I'm not sure," he answered. "Maybe if we're extra good, that will stop them."

"Or we get in trouble," said the Sister thoughtfully, "that might work too."

With jokes and stories, the children could make their parents laugh, just not with each other. Acts of mischief didn't help much either. When one parent grew, the other shrank. Faces flashed or turned away.

At night-time, cold draughts travelled upstairs. The Brother and Sister stared at each other, not sure what else to say or do. The sky was turning darker, the winds stronger.

One day, the children returned from school in time to see a jagged bolt of lightning hit their treehouse and break it in two.

"No!" cried the Brother, blinking back tears. "Our family home … where we grew up!"

"Why, oh why has this happened?" wailed the Sister, hand clasped to her mouth. "Where are you … Mum, Dad?"

Mum and Dad stood on either side of their home, faces long and worn, hard to recognise. A deep crack tore through the treehouse, right down to its roots. Furniture and toys spilled onto the garden, some into the earth itself.

From either side their parents spoke, voices low, almost a whisper, "We are no longer going to live together, we are separating. We are sorry. Just remember, it's not your fault, any of this."

Heads spinning, the Brother and Sister rushed through the gate. In their confusion, they didn't see the broken ground beneath their feet. Tumbling through the crack, they landed at its bottom where the oldest, deepest roots lay.

Stunned into silence, they peered up at their Mum and Dad, whose voices they could hardly hear. Down here in the dark, shadows threw strange shapes.

"How do we get back home?" whispered the Sister finally, as she stood up to run her hands along the crack.

"I don't know," said the Brother, curling up into a ball, not wanting to move anywhere.

"You've had a crash landing," called out a voice from behind. "A terrible shock, eh."

The children froze, their eyes wide. A huge Firebird with flaming feathers lit up the pit where they had fallen.

Now they had light, the children could see a few objects that had fallen here too: old toys, books and family photos, all theirs. The Brother and Sister held their breath as the Firebird began turning over each object with its beak. It moved with such purpose.

"Can you mend broken things," asked the Brother, heart swelling with hope, "by magic?"

The Firebird had picked something from the floor. It was a photo of their parents, torn in two. Tears pricked at the children's eyes.

"Some things break beyond repair," answered the Firebird softly, its wings suddenly not so bright anymore, "but your memories, what you want to remember, they don't have to."

A wave of feeling, hot and cold, crashed into each child's heart. Far above, they could hear faint voices, Mum and Dad calling down, trying to reassure them.

"Well, if you can't fix anything," cried the Sister, cheeks burning, "can you at least help us get out of here?"

The Firebird seemed to lose even more shine as it dropped one half of the photo into each child's hand, "Hold on to these, however hard it gets, and I can show you the way out."

"I've got Dad," said the Brother, tears running down his cheeks.

"I never thought our family would split like this," the Sister replied, voice choking up, as she held up the picture of Mum.

"What's going to happen to us?" said the Brother.

Behind them, the Firebird opened its wings, its feathers no longer blazing but flickering like candles. Even so, the children spotted it straightaway. Among the tangle of roots in the earthy wall was a ladder leading upwards. Far above, Mum and Dad called down from their separate sides. Looking at their photos, the children's eyes flashed with the same idea.

"We'll take turns with Mum and Dad," cried out the Sister, "see them one at a time."

"Keep a piece of them," said her Brother, tucking the photo with care into a pocket.

"Yes ... Mum will always be Mum, and Dad our Dad," said the Sister, "even if they're not together."

"That's one thing that doesn't change," added the Brother solemnly.

By the dim glow of the Firebird, the children climbed upwards. They kept on going, even when their arms and legs became sore, their hearts impossibly heavy. The light from the Firebird had nearly gone out, its feathers dark and dusty.

Just as they neared the top, there was a loud fizzing noise and, without warning, the Firebird exploded into flames. The children gasped. Far from burning out, the Firebird shone as brightly as before. It lifted its head and sang out,

Remember, whatever you feel, is right and true,

A response to losing what's important to you.

Like all storms, with enough time, it will pass ...

And after, you can try and make something new.

With a final wave and burst of light, the Firebird dived back inside the crack. The children threw themselves out on the grass outside.

Mum and Dad knelt on either side, relieved to see them and looking just as worn out as the children felt. Across the gap, a few fallen branches had been dragged — a makeshift bridge.

"I guess our family is going to have a different shape now," said the Brother.

"Yes," answered his Sister, as she started across the tree-bridge, arms out, wobbling. "Whatever happens, whatever we make, it's going to be a different shape ... for each of us too."